THE MAN THE MARTIANS MADE

THE MAN THE MARTIANS MADE

by Frank Belknap Long

I

No mortal had ever seen the Martians, but they had heard their whisperings without knowing the terrible secret they kept hidden.

There was death in the camp.

I knew when I awoke that it had come to stand with us in the night and was waiting now for the day to break and flood the desert with light. There was a prickling at the base of my scalp and I was drenched with cold sweat.

I had an impulse to leap up and go stumbling about in the darkness. But I disciplined myself. I crossed my arms and waited for the sky to grow bright.

Daybreak on Mars is like nothing you've ever dreamed about. You wake up in the morning, and there it is bright and clear and shining. You pinch yourself, you sit up straight, but it doesn't vanish.

Then you stare at your hands with the big callouses. You reach for a mirror to take a look at your face. That's not so good. That's where ugliness enters the picture. You look around and you see Ralph. You see Harry. You see the women.

On Earth a woman may not look her glamorous best in the harsh light of early dawn, but if she's really beautiful she doesn't look too bad. On Mars even the most beautiful woman looks angry on arising, too weary and tormented by human shortcomings to take a prefabricated metal shack and turn it into a real home for a man.

You have to make allowances for a lot of things on Mars. You have to start right off by accepting hardship and privation as your daily lot. You have to get accustomed to living in construction camps in the desert, with the red dust making you feel all hollow and dried up inside. Making you feel like a drum, a shriveled pea pod, a salted fish hung up to dry. Dust inside of you, rattling around, canal water seepage rotting the soles of your boots.

THE MAN THE MARTIANS MADE

So you wake up and you stare. The night before you'd collected driftwood and stacked it by the fire. The driftwood has disappeared. Someone has stolen your very precious driftwood. The Martians? Guess again.

You get up and you walk straight up to Ralph with your shoulders squared. You say, "Ralph, why in hell did you have to steal my driftwood?"

In your mind you say that. You say it to Dick, you say it to Harry. But what you really say is, "Larsen was here again last night!"

You say, I put a fish on to boil and Larsen ate it. I had a nice deck of cards, all shiny and new, and Larsen marked them up. It wasn't me cheating. It was Larsen hoping I'd win so that he could waylay me in the desert and get all of the money away from me.

You have a girl. There aren't too many girls in the camps with laughter and light and fire in them. But there are a few, and if you're lucky you take a fancy to one particular girl her full red lips and her spun gold hair. All of a sudden she disappears. Somebody runs off with her. It's Larsen.

In every man there is a slumbering giant. When life roars about you on a world that's rugged and new you've got to go on respecting the lads who have thrown in their lot with you, even when their impulses are as harsh as the glint of sunlight on a desert-polished tombstone.

You think of a name: Larsen. You start from scratch and you build Larsen up until you have a clear picture of him in your mind. You build him up until he's a great shouting, brawling, golden man like Paul Bunyon.

Even a wicked legend can seem golden on Mars. Larsen wasn't just my slumbering giantCor Dick's, or Harry's. He was the slumbering giant in all of us, and that's what made him so tremendous. Anything gigantic has beauty and power and drive to it.

Alone we couldn't do anything with Larsen's gusto, so when some great act of wickedness was done with gusto how could it be us? Here comes Larsen! He'll shoulder all the guilt, but he won't feel guilty because he's the first man in Eden, the child who never grew up, the laughing boy, Hercules balancing the world on his shoulders and looking for a woman with long shining tresses and eyes like the stars of heaven to bend to his will.

If such a woman came to life in Hercules' arms would you like the job of stopping him from sending the world crashing? Would you care to try?

Don't you see? Larsen was closer to us than breathing and as necessary as food and drink and our dreams of a brighter tomorrow. Don't think we didn't hate him at times. Don't think we didn't curse and revile him. You may glorify a legend from here to eternity, but the luster never remains completely untarnished.

Larsen wouldn't have seemed completely real to us if we hadn't given him muscles that could tire and eyes that could blink shut in weariness. Larsen had to sleep, just as we did. He'd disappear for days.

We'd wink and say, "Larsen's getting a good long rest this time. But he'll be back with something new up his sleeve, don't you worry!"

We could joke about it, sure. When Larsen stole or cheated we could pretend we were playing a game with loaded dice not really a deadly game, but a game full of sound and fury with a great rousing outburst of merriment at the end of it.

But there are deadlier games by far. I lay motionless, my arms locked across my chest, sweating from every pore. I stared at Harry. We'd been working all night digging a well, and in a few days water would be bubbling up sweet and cool and we wouldn't have to go to the canal to fill our cooking utensils. Harry was blinking and stirring and I could tell just by looking at him that he was uneasy too. I looked beyond him at the circle of shacks.

Most of us were sleeping in the open, but there were a few youngsters in the shacks and women too worn out with drudgery to care much whether they slept in smothering darkness or under the clear cold light of the stars.

I got slowly to my knees, scooped up a handful of sand, and let it dribble slowly through my fingers. Harry looked straight at me and his eyes widened in alarm. It must have been the look on my face. He arose and crossed to where I was sitting, his mouth twitching slightly. There was nothing very reassuring about Harry. Life had not been kind to him and he had resigned himself to accepting the slings and arrows of outrageous fortune without protest. He had one of those emaciated, almost skull-like faces which terrify children, and make women want to cry.

"You don't look well, Tom," he said. "You've been driving yourself too hard."

I looked away quickly. I had to tell him, but anything terrifying could demoralize Harry and make him throw his arm before his face in blind panic. But I couldn't keep it locked up inside me an instant longer.

"Sit down, Harry," I whispered. "I want to talk to you. No sense in waking the others."

"Oh," he said.

He squatted beside me on the sand, his eyes searching my face. "What is it, Tom?"

"I heard a scream," I said. "It was pretty awful. Somebody has been hurt bad. It woke me up, and that takes some doing."

Harry nodded. "You sleep like a log," he said.

"I just lay still and listened," I said, "with my eyes wide open. Something moved out from the well a two-legged something. It didn't make a sound. It was big, Harry, and it seemed to melt into the shadows. I don't know what kept me from leaping up and going after it. It had something to do with the way I felt. All frozen up inside."

Harry appeared to understand. He nodded, his eyes darting toward the well. "How long ago was that?"

"Ten, fifteen minutes."

"You just waited for me to wake up?"

"That's right," I said. "There was something about the scream that made me want to put off finding out. Two's company and when you're alone with something like that it's best to talk it over before you act."

I could see that Harry was pleased. Unnerved too, and horribly shaken. But he was pleased that I had turned to him as a friend I could trust. When you can't depend on life for anything else it's good to know you have a friend.

I brushed sand from my trousers and got up. "Come on," I said. "We'll take a look."

FRANK BELKNAP LONG

It was an ordeal for him. His face twitched and his eyes wavered. He knew I hadn't lied about the scream. If a single scream could unnerve me that much it had to be bad.

We walked to the well in complete silence. There were shadows everywhere, chill and forbidding. Almost like people they seemed, whispering together, huddling close in ominous gossipy silence, aware of what we would find.

It was a sixty-foot walk from the fire to the well. A walk in the sun, a walk in the bright hot sun of Mars, with utter horror perhaps at the end of it.

The horror was there. Harry made a little choking noise deep in his throat, and my heart started pounding like a bass drum.

II

The man on the sand had no top to his head. His skull had been crushed and flattened so hideously that he seemed like a wooden figure resting there, an anatomical dummy with its skull-case lifted off.

We looked around for the skull-case, hoping we'd find it, hoping we'd made a mistake and stumbled by accident into an open-air dissecting laboratory and were looking at ghastly props made of plastic and glittering metal instead of bone and muscle and flesh.

But the man on the sand had a name. We'd known him for weeks and talked to him. He wasn't a medical dummy, but a corpse. His limbs were hideously convulsed, his eyes wide and staring. The sand beneath his head was clotted with dried blood. We looked for the weapon which had crushed his skull but couldn't find it.

We looked for the weapon before we saw the footprints in the sand. Big they were incredibly large and massive. A man with a size-twelve shoe might have left such prints if the leather had become a little soggy and spread out around the soles.

"The poor guy," Harry whispered.

I knew how he felt. We had all liked Ned. A harmless little guy with a great love of solitude, a guy who hadn't a malicious hair in his head. A happy little guy who liked to sing and dance in the light of a high-leaping fire. He had a banjo and was good at music making. Who could have hated Ned with a rage so primitive and savage? I looked at Harry and saw that he was wondering the same thing.

Harry looked pretty bad, about ready to cave in. He was leaning against the well, a tormented fury in his eyes.

"The murderous bastard," he muttered. "I'd like to get him by the throat and choke the breath out of him. Who'd want to do a thing like that to Ned."

"I can't figure it either," I said.

Then I remembered. I don't think Molly Egan really could have loved Ned. The curious thing about it was that Ned didn't even need the kind of love she could have given him. He was a self-sufficient little guy despite his frailness and didn't really need a woman to look after him. But Molly must have seen something pathetic in him.

Molly was a beautiful woman in her own right, and there wasn't a man in the camp who hadn't envied Ned. It was puzzling, but it could have explained why Ned was lying slumped on the sand with a bashed-in skull. It could have explained why someone had hated him enough to kill him.

Without lifting a finger Ned had won Molly's love. That could make some other guy as mad as a caged hyena, the wrong sort of other guy. Even a small man could have shattered Ned's skull, but the prints on the sand were big.

How many men in the camp wore size-twelve shoes? That was the sixty-four dollar question, and it hung in the shimmering air between Harry and myself like an unspoken challenge. We could almost see the curve of the big question mark suspended in the dazzle.

I thought awhile, looking at Harry. Then I took a long, deep breath and said, "We'd better talk it over with Bill Seaton first. If it gets around too fast those footprints will be trampled flat. And if tempers start rising anything could happen."

Harry nodded. Bill was the kind of guy you could depend on in an emergency. Cool, poised, efficient, with an air of authority that commanded respect. He could be pigheaded at times, but his sense of justice was as keen as a whip.

Harry and I walked very quietly across a stretch of tumbled sand and halted at the door to Bill's shack. Bill was a bachelor and we knew there'd be no woman inside to put her foot down and tell him he'd be a fool to act as a lawman. Or would there be? We had to chance it.

Law-enforcement is a thankless job whether on Earth or on Mars. That's why it attracts the worst and the best. If you're a power-drunk sadist you'll take the job just for the pleasure it gives you. But if you're really interested in keeping violence within bounds so that fairly decent lads get a fighting chance to build for the future, you'll take the job with no thought of reward beyond the simple satisfaction of lending a helping hand.

Bill Seaton was such a man, even if he did enjoy the limelight and liked to be in a position of command.

"Come on, Harry," I said. "We may as well wake him up and get it over with."

We went into the shack. Bill was sleeping on the floor with his long legs drawn up. His mouth was open and he was snoring lustily. I couldn't help thinking how much he looked like an overgrown grasshopper. But that was just a first impression springing from overwrought nerves.

I bent down and shook Bill awake. I grabbed his arm and shook him until his jaw snapped shut and he shot up straight, suddenly galvanized. Instantly the grotesque aspect fell from him. Dignity came upon him and enveloped him like a cloak.

"Ned, you say? The poor little cuss! So help me if I get my hands on the rat who did it I'll roast him over a slow fire!"

He got up, staggered to an equipment locker, and took out a sun helmet and a pair of shorts. He dressed quickly, swearing constantly and staring out the door at the bright dawn glow as if he wanted to send both of his fists crashing into the first suspicious guy to cross his path.

"We can't have those footprints trampled," he muttered. "There are a lot of dumb bastards here who don't know the first thing about keeping pointers intact. Those prints may be the only thing we'll have to go on."

"Just the three of us can handle it, Bill," I said. "When you decide what should be done we can wake the others."

Bill nodded. "Keeping it quiet is the important thing. We'll carry him back here. When we break the news I want that body out of sight."

Harry and Bill and I, we took another walk in the sun. I looked at Harry, and the greenish tinge which had crept into his face gave me a jolt. He's taking this pretty hard, I thought. If I hadn't known him so well I might have jumped to an ugly conclusion. But I just couldn't imagine Harry quarreling with Ned over Molly.

How was I taking it myself? I raised my hand and looked at it. There was no tremor. Nerves steady, brain clear. No pleasure in enforcing the law pass that buck to Bill. But there was a gruesome job ahead, and I was standing up to it as well as could be expected.

Ever try lifting a corpse? The corpse of a stranger is easier to lift than the corpse of a man you've known and liked. Harry and I lifted him together. Between us the dead weight didn't seem too intolerable, not at first. But it quickly became a terrible, heavy limpness that dragged at our arms like some soggy log dredged up from the dark waters of the canal.

We carried him into the shack and eased him down on the floor. His head fell back and his eyes lolled.

Death is always shameful. It strips away all human reticences and makes a mockery of human dignity and man's rebellion against the cruelty of fate.

For a moment we stood staring down at all that was left of Ned. I looked at Bill. "How many men in the camp wear number-twelve shoes?"

"We'll find out soon enough."

All this time we hadn't mentioned Larsen. Not one word about Larsen, not one spoken word. Cheating, yes. Lying, and treacherous disloyalty, and viciousness, and spite. Fights around the campfires at midnight, battered faces and broken wrists and a cursing that never ceased. All that we could blame on Larsen. But a harmless little guy lying dead by a well in a spreading pool of blood that was an outrage that stopped us dead in our legend-making tracks.

There is something in the human mind which recoils from too outrageous a deception. How wonderful it would have been to say, "Larsen was here again last night. He found a little guy who had never harmed anyone standing by a well in the moonlight. Just for sheer delight he decided to kill the little guy right then and there." Just to add luster to the legend, just to send a thrill of excitement about the camp.

No, that would have been the lie colossal which no sane man could have quite believed.

Something happened then to further unnerve us.

The most disturbing sound you can hear on Mars is the whispering. Usually it begins as a barely audible murmur and swells in volume with every shift of the wind. But now it started off high pitched and insistent and did not stop.

It was the whispering of a dying race. The Martians are as elusive as elves and all the pitiless logic of science had failed to draw them forth into the sunlight to stand before men in uncompromising arrogance as peers of the human race.

That failure was a tragedy in itself. If man's supremacy is to be challenged at all let it be by a creature of flesh-and-blood, a big-brained biped who must kill to live. Better that by far than a ghostly flickering in the deepening dusk, a whispering and a flapping and a long-drawn sighing prophesying death.

Oh, the Martians were real enough. A flitting vampire bat is real, or a stinging ray in the depths of a blue lagoon. But who could point to a Martian and say, "I have seen you plain, in broad daylight. I have looked into your owlish eyes and watched you go flitting over the sand on your thin, stalklike legs? I know there is nothing mysterious about you. You are like a water insect skimming the surface of a pond in a familiar meadow on Earth. You are quick and alert, but no match for a man. You are no more than an interesting insect."

Who could say that, when there were ruins buried deep beneath the sand to give the lie to any such idea. First the ruins, and then the Martians themselves, always elusive, gnomelike, goblinlike, flitting away into the dissolving dusk.

You're a comparative archaeologist and you're on Mars with the first batch of rugged youngsters to come tumbling out of a spaceship with stardust in their eyes. You see those youngsters digging wells and sweating in the desert. You see the prefabricated housing units go up, the tangle of machinery, the camp sites growing lusty with midnight brawls and skull-cracking escapades. You see the towns in the desert, the law-enforcement committees, the camp followers, the reform fanatics.

You're a sober-minded scholar, so you start digging in the ruins. You bring up odd-looking cylinders, rolls of threaded film, instruments of science so complex they make you giddy.

You wonder about the Martians, what they were like when they were a young and proud race. If you're an archaeologist you wonder. But Bill and I, we were youngsters still. Oh, sure, we were in our thirties, but who would have suspected that? Bill looked twenty-seven and I hadn't a gray hair in my head.

III

Bill nodded at Harry. "You'd better stay here. Tom and I will be asking some pointed questions, and our first move will depend on the answers we get. Don't let anyone come snooping around this shack. If anyone sticks his head in and starts to turn ugly, warn him just once then shoot to kill." He handed Harry a gun.

Harry nodded grimly and settled himself on the floor close to Ned. For the first time since I'd known him, Harry looked completely sure of himself.

As we emerged from the shack the whispering was so loud the entire camp had been placed on the alert. There would be no need for us to go into shack after shack, watching surprise and shock come into their eyes.

A dozen or more men were between Bill's shack and the well. They were staring grimly at the dawn, as if they could already see blood on the sky, spilling over on the sand and spreading out in a sinister pool at their feet. A mirage-like pool mirroring their own hidden forebodings, mirroring a knotted rope and the straining shoulders of men too vengeful to know the meaning of restraint.

Jim Kenny stood apart and alone, about forty feet from the well, staring straight at us. His shirt was open at the throat, exposing a patch of hairy chest, and his big hands were wedged deeply into his belt. He stood about six feet three, very powerful, and with large feet.

I nudged Bill's arm. "What do you think?" I asked.

Kenny did seem a likely suspect. Molly had caught his eye right from the start, and he had lost no time in pursuing her. A guy like Kenny would have felt that losing out to a man of his own breed would have been a terrible blow to his pride. But just imagine Kenny losing out to a little guy like Ned. It would have infuriated him and glazed his eyes with a red film of hate.

Bill answered my question slowly, his eyes on Kenny's cropped head. "I think we'd better take a look at his shoes," he said.

We edged up slowly, taking care not to disturb the others, pretending we were sauntering toward the well on a before-breakfast stroll.

It was then that Molly came out of her shack. She stood blinking for an instant in the dawn glare, her unbound hair falling in a tumbled dark mass to her shoulders, her eyes still drowsy with sleep. She wore rust-colored slippers and a form-fitted yellow robe, belted in at the waist.

Molly wasn't beautiful exactly. But there was something pulse-stirring about her and it was easy to understand how a man like Kenny might find her difficult to resist.

Bill slanted a glance at Kenny, then shrugged and looked straight at Molly. He turned to me, his voice almost a whisper, "She's got to be told, Tom. You do it. She likes you a lot."

I'd been wondering about that myself just how much she liked me. It was hard to be sure.

Bill saw my hesitation, and frowned. "You can tell if she's covering up. Her reaction may give us a lead."

Molly looked startled when she saw me approaching without the mask I usually wore when I waltzed her around and grinned and ruffled her hair and told her that she was the cutest kid imaginable and would make some man, not me, a fine wife.

That made telling her all the harder. The hardest part was at the end when she stared at me dry-eyed and threw her arms around me as if I was the last support left to her on Earth.

For a moment I almost forgot we were not on Earth. On Earth I might have been able to comfort her in a completely sane way. But on Mars when a woman comes into your arms your emotions can turn molten in a matter of seconds.

"Steady," I whispered. "We're just good friends, remember?"

"I'd be willing to forget, Tom," she said.

"You've had a terrible shock," I whispered. "You really loved that little guy more than you know. It's natural enough that you should feel a certain warmth toward me. I just happened to be here so you kissed me."

"No, Tom. It isn't that way at all!"

THE MAN THE MARTIANS MADE

I might have let myself go a little then if Kenny hadn't seen us. He stood very still for an instant, staring at Molly. Then his eyes narrowed and he walked slowly toward us, his hands still wedged in his belt.

I looked quickly at Molly, and saw that her features had hardened. There was a look of dark suspicion in her eyes. Bill had been watching Kenny, too, waiting for him to move. He measured footsteps with Kenny, advancing in the same direction from a different angle at a pace so calculated that they seemed to meet by accident directly in front of us.

Bill didn't draw but his hand never left his hip. His voice came clear and sharp and edged with cold insistence. "Know anything about it, Kenny?"

Strain seemed to tighten Kenny's face, but there was no panic in his eyes, no actual glint of fear. "What made you think I'd know?" he asked.

Bill didn't say a word. He just started staring at Kenny's shoes. He stood back a bit and continued to stare as if something vitally important had escaped him and taken refuge beneath the soggy leather around Kenny's feet.

"What size shoes do you wear, Jim?" he asked.

Kenny must have suspected that the question was charged with as much explosive risk as a detonating wire set to go off at the faintest jar. His eyes grew shrewd and mocking.

"So the guy who did it left prints in the sand?" he said. "Prints made by big shoes?"

"That's right," Bill said. "You have a very active mind."

Kenny laughed then, the mockery deepening in his stare. "Well," he said, "suppose we have a look at those prints, and if it will ease your mind I'll take off my shoes and you can try them out for size."

Kenny and Bill and I walked slowly from Molly's shack to the well in the hot and blazing glare, and the whispering went right on, getting under our skin in a tormenting sort of way.

Kenny still wore that disturbing grin. He looked at the prints and grunted. "Yeah," he said, "they sure are big. Biggest prints I've ever seen."

He sat down and started unlacing his shoes. First the right shoe, then the left. He pulled off both shoes and handed them to Bill.

18

"Fit them in," he said. "Measure them for size. Measure *me* for size, and to hell with you!"

Bill made a careful check. There were eight prints, and he fitted the shoes painstakingly into each of them. There was space to spare at each try.

It cleared Kenny completely. He wasn't a killerCthis time. We might have roused the camp to a lynching fury and Kenny would have died for a crime another man had committed. I shut my eyes and saw Larsen swinging from a roof top, a black hood over his face. I saw Molly standing in the sunlight by my side, her face a stony mask.

I opened my eyes and there was Kenny, grinning contemptuously at us. He'd called our bluff and won out. Now the shoe was on the other foot.

A cold chill ran up my spine. It was Kenny who was doing the staring now, and he was looking directly at my shoes. He stood back a bit and continued to stare. He was dramatizing his sudden triumph in a way that turned my blood to ice.

Then I saw that Bill was staring too straight at the shoes of a man he had known for three years and grown to like and trust. But underlying the warmth and friendliness in Bill was a granite-like integrity which nothing could shake.

It was Bill who spoke first. "I guess you'd better take them off, Tom," he said. "We may as well be thorough about this."

Sure, I was big. I grew up fast as a kid and at eighteen I weighed two hundred and thirty pounds, all lean flesh. If shoes ran large I could sometimes cram my feet into size twelves, but I felt much more comfortable in a size or two larger than that.

What made it worse, Molly liked me. I was involved with her, but no one knew how much. No one knew whether we'd quarreled or not, or how insanely jealous I could be. No one knew whether Molly had only pretended to like Ned while carrying a torch for me, and how dangerously complex the situation might have become all along the line.

I stood very still, listening. The whispering was so loud now it drowned out the sighing of the wind. I looked down at my shoes. They were caked with mud and soggy and discolored. Day after day I'd trudge back and forth from the canal to the shacks in the blazing sunlight without giving my feet a thought until the ache in them had become intolerable, rest an absolute necessity.

There was only one thing to do, call Kenny's bluff so fast he wouldn't have time to hurl another accusation at me.

I handed Bill both of my shoes. He looked at me and nodded. I waited, listening to the whispering rise and fall, watching him stoop and fit the shoes into the prints on the sand.

He straightened suddenly. His face was expressionless, but I could see that he was waging a terrible inward struggle with himself.

"Your shoes come pretty close to filling out those prints, Tom," he said. "I can't be sure, but a wax impression test should pretty well clear this up." He gripped my arm and nodded toward the shacks. "Better stick close to me."

Kenny took a slow step backward, his jaw tightening, his eyes searching Bill's face. "Wax impression test, hell!" he said. "You've got your murderer. I'm going to see he gets what's coming to him right now!"

Bill shook his head. "I'll do this my way," he said.

Kenny glared at him, then laughed harshly. "You won't have a chance," he said. "The boys won't stand for it. I'm going to spread the word around, and you'd better not try to stop me."

That did it. I'd been holding myself in, but I had a sudden, overpowering urge to send my fist crashing into Kenny's face, to send him crashing to the sand. I started for him, but he jumped back and started shouting.

I can't remember exactly what he shouted. But he said just enough to put a noose around my neck. Every man and woman between the shacks and the well swung about to stare at me. I saw shock and rage flare in the eyes of men who usually had steady nerves. They were not calm now, not one of them.

IV

It all happened so fast I was caught off balance. In the harsh Martian sunlight human emotions can be as unstable as a wind-lashed dune.

A crazy thought flashed through my mind: Will Molly believe this too? Will she join these madmen in their wild thirst for vengeance? My need for her was suddenly overwhelming. Just seeing her face would have helped, but now more men had emerged from the shacks and I couldn't see beyond them. They were heading straight for me and I knew that even Bill would be powerless to stop them.

You can't argue with an avalanche. It was rolling straight toward me, gathering momentum as it came, not one man or a dozen, but a solid wall of human hate and unreason.

Bill stood his ground. He had drawn his gun, and he started shouting that the prints couldn't have been made by my shoes. I chalked that up to his credit and resolved never to forget it.

I knew I'd have to make a dash for it. I ran as fast as I could, keeping my eyes on the glimmer of sunlight on rising dunes, and deep hollows which a carefully placed bullet could have quickly changed into a burial mound.

A sudden crackling burst of gunfire ripped through the air. Directly in my path the sand geysered up as the bullets ripped and tore at it. Somebody wasn't a good marksman, or had let blind rage unnerve him and spoil his aim. A lot of somebodies for the firing increased and became almost continuous for an instant, a dull crackling which drowned out the whispering and the sighing of the wind.

Then abruptly all sound ceased. Utter stillness descended on the desert an unnatural, terrifying stillness, as if nature herself had stopped breathing and was waiting for someone to scream.

I must have been mad to turn. A weaving target has a chance, but a target standing motionless is a sitting duck and his life hangs by a hair. But still I turned.

THE MAN THE MARTIANS MADE

Something was happening between the well and the shacks which halted the pursuit dead in its tracks. One of the shacks was wrapped in darting tongues of flame, and a woman was screaming, and a man close to her was grappling with something huge and misshapen which loomed starkly against the dawn glow.

A human shape? I could not be sure. It seemed monstrous, with a bulge between its shoulders which gave a grotesque and distorted aspect to the shadow which its weaving bulk cast upon the sand. I could see the shadow clearly across three hundred feet of sand. It lengthened and shortened, as if an octopus-like ferocity had given it the power to distort itself at will, lengthening its tentacles and then whipping them back again.

But it was not an octopus. It had legs and arms, and it was crushing the man in a grip of steel. I could see that now. I stared as the others were staring, their backs turned to me, their blind hatred for me blotted out by that greater horror.

I suddenly realized that the shape was human. It had the head and shoulders of a man, and a torso that could twist with muscular purpose, and massive hands that could maul and maim. It threw the hapless man from it with a sudden convulsive contraction of its entire bulk. I had never seen a human being move in quite that way, but even as its violence flared its manlike aspect became more pronounced.

A frightful thing happened then. The woman screamed and rushed toward the brutish maniac with her fingers splayed. The swaying figure bent, grabbed her about the waist, and lifted her high into the air. I thought for a moment he was about to crush her as he had crushed the man. But I was wrong. She was hurled to the sand, but with a violence so brutal that she went instantly limp.

Then the brutal madman turned, and I saw his face. If ever monstrous cruelty and malign cunning looked out of a human countenance it looked out of the eyes that stared in my direction, remorseless in their hate.

I could not tear my gaze from his face. The hate in it could be sensed, even across a blinding haze of sunlight that blotted out the sharp contours of physical things. But more than hate could be sensed. There was something tremendous about that face, as if the evil which had ravaged it had left the searing brand of Lucifer himself!

For an instant the madman stood motionless, his ghastly brutality unchallenged. Then Jeff Winters started for it. Jeff had come to Mars alone and grown more solitary with every passing day. He was a brooding, ingrown man, secretive and sullen, with a streak of wildness which he usually managed to control. He went for the madman like a gigantic terrier pup, shaggy and ferocious and contemptuous of death.

The big figure turned quickly, raised his arm, and brought his closed fist down on Jeff's skull. Jeff collapsed like a shattered plaster cast. His body seemed to break and splinter, and he sprawled forward on the sand.

He did not get up.

Frank Anders had guns on both hips, and he drew them fast. No one knew what kind of man Anders was. He hardly ever complained or made a spectacle of himself. A little guy with sandy hair and cold blue eyes, he had an accuracy of aim that did his talking for him.

His guns suddenly roared. For an instant the air between his hands and the maniac was a crackling wall of flame. The brute swayed a little but did not turn aside. He went straight for Anders with both arms spread wide.

He caught Anders about the waist, lifted him up, and slammed his body down against the sand. A sickness came over me as I stared. The madman bashed Anders' head against the ground again and again. Then suddenly the big arms relaxed and Anders sagged limply to the ground.

For an instant the madman swayed slowly back and forth, like a blood-stained marionette on a wire. Then he moved forward with a terrible, shambling gait, his head lowered, a dark, misshapen shadow seeming to lengthen before him on the sand like a spindle of flame.

The clearing was abruptly tumultuous with sound. The fury which had been unleashed against me turned upon the monster and became a closed circle of deadly, intent purpose hemming him in and he was caught in a crossfire that hurled him backwards to the sand.

23

THE MAN THE MARTIANS MADE

He jumped up and lunged straight for the well. What happened then was like the awakening stages of some horrible dream. The madman shambled past the well, the air at his back a crackling sheet of flame. The barrage behind him was continuous and merciless. The men were organized now, standing together in a solid wall, firing with deadly accuracy and a grim purpose which transcended fear.

The madman went clumping on past me and climbed a dune with his shoulders held straight. With a sunset glare deepening about him, he went striding over the dune and out of sight.

*

I turned and stared back at the camp. The pursuit had passed the well and was headed for me. But no one paid the slightest attention to me. Twelve men passed me, walking three abreast. Bill came along in their wake, his eyes stony hard. He reached out as he passed me, gripping my shoulder, giving me a foot-of-the-gallows kind of smile.

"We know now who killed Ned," he whispered. "We know, fella. Take it easy, relax."

My head was throbbing, but I could see the big prints from where I stood the prints of a murderer betrayed by his insatiable urge to slay.

I saw Kenny pass, and he gave me a contemptuous grin. He had done his best to destroy me, but there was no longer any hate left in me.

I took a slow step forward and fell flat on my face....

I woke up with my head in Molly's lap. She was looking down into my face, sobbing in a funny sort of way and running her fingers through my hair.

She looked startled when she saw that I was wide awake. She blinked furiously and started fumbling at her waist for a handkerchief.

"I must have passed out cold," I said. "It's quite a strain to be at the receiving end of a lynching bee. And what I saw afterwards wasn't exactly pleasant."

"Darling," she whispered, "don't move, don't say a word. You're going to be all right."

"You bet I am!" I said. "Right now I feel great."

My arm went around her shoulder, and I drew her head down until her breath was warm on my face. I kissed her hair and lips and eyes for a full minute in utter recklessness.

When I released her her eyes were shining, and she was laughing a little and crying too. "You've changed your mind," she said. "You believe me now, don't you?"

"Don't talk," I said. "Don't say another word. I just want to look at you."

"It was you right from the start," she said. "Not Ned or anyone else."

"I was a blind fool," I said.

"You never gave me a second glance."

"One glance was enough," I whispered. "But when I saw how it seemed to be between you and Ned."

"I was never in love with him. It was just—"

"Never mind, don't say it," I said. "It's over and done with."

I stopped, remembering. Her eyes grew wide and startled, and I could see that she was remembering too.

"What happened?" I asked. "Did they catch that vicious rat?"

She brushed back her hair, the sunlight suddenly harsh on her face. "He fell into the canal. The bullets brought him down, and he collapsed on the bank."

Her hand tightened on my wrist. "Bill told me. He tried to swim, but the current carried him under. He went down and never came up."

"I'm glad," I said. "Did anyone in the camp ever see him before?"

Molly shook her head. "Bill said he was a drifter a dangerous maniac who must have been crazed by the sun."

"I see," I said.

I reached out and drew her into my arms again, and we rested for a moment stretched out side by side on the sand.

"It's funny," I said after a while.

"What is?"

THE MAN THE MARTIANS MADE

"You know what they say about the whispering. Sometimes when you listen intently you seem to hear words deep in your mind. As if the Martians had telepathic powers."

"Perhaps they have," she said.

I glanced sideways at her. "Remember," I said. "There were cities on Mars when our ancestors were hairy apes. The Martian civilization was flourishing and great fifty million years before the pyramids arose as a monument to human solidarity and worth. A bad monument, built by slave labor. But at least it was a start."

"Now you're being poetic, Tom," she said.

"Perhaps I am. The Martians must have had their pyramids too. And at the pyramid stage they must have had their Larsens, to shoulder all the guilt. To them we may still be in the pyramid stage. Suppose—"

"Suppose what?"

"Suppose they wanted to warn us, to give us a lesson we couldn't forget. How can we say with certainty that a dying race couldn't still make use of certain techniques that are far beyond us."

"I'm afraid I don't understand," she said, puzzled.

"Someday," I said, "our own science will take a tiny fragment of human tissue from the body of a dead man, put it into an incubating machine, and a new man will arise again from that tiny shred of flesh. A man who can walk and live and breathe again, and love again, and die again after another full lifetime.

"Perhaps the Martian science was once as great as that. And the Martians might still remember a few of the techniques. Perhaps from our human brains, from our buried memories and desires, they could filch the key and bring to horrible life a thing so monstrous and so terrible—"

Her hand went suddenly cold in mine. "Tom, you can't honestly think—"

"No," I said. "It's nonsense, of course. Forget it."

I didn't tell her what the whispering had seemed to say, deep in my mind.

FRANK BELKNAP LONG

We've brought you Larsen! You wanted Larsen, and we've made him for you! His flesh and his mind his cruel strength and his wicked heart! Here he comes, here he is! Larsen, Larsen, Larsen!